Are we there yet?

Alison Lester

A journey around Australia

PENGUIN | VIKING

Starting out

The year I turned eight, Mum and Dad took us on a trip around Australia. Luke, Billy and I missed school for the whole winter term.

Nan and Poppa stayed behind to look after Buffy and Tigger and Bess.

We towed Poppa's old camper trailer, and it was our home for three months. It folded out to make a little house, with a table, a fridge, two double beds, a stove and a sink. It had everything we needed.

For my travelling companions, Eddy, Will, Clair and Lach

This book took a decade to reach publication.
Thanks to Rita Hart for sticking with it all the way.

VIKING

UK | USA | Canada | Ireland | Australia
India | New Zealand | South Africa | China

Penguin Books is part of the Penguin Random House group of companies
whose addresses can be found at global.penguinrandomhouse.com.

First published in hardback by Penguin Group (Australia), 2004
This edition published by Penguin Random House Australia Pty Ltd, 2016

Cover and text design by Susannah Low & Deborah Brash © Penguin Random House Australia Pty Ltd
Typeset in 15.5/20.5pt Minion by Deborah Brash
Colour separation by Splitting Image Colour Studio, Clayton, Victoria
Printed and bound in China

National Library of Australia Cataloguing-in-Publication data:

Lester, Alison.
Are we there yet?
ISBN 978 0 670 88067 6
1. Australia – description and travel – Juvenile fiction
I. Title

A823.3

penguin.com.au

We practised in the backyard before we left

Cross-section of our van

Luke slept in his swag under the stars except when it rained, and then he bunked in with us. We were squashed but it was cosy.

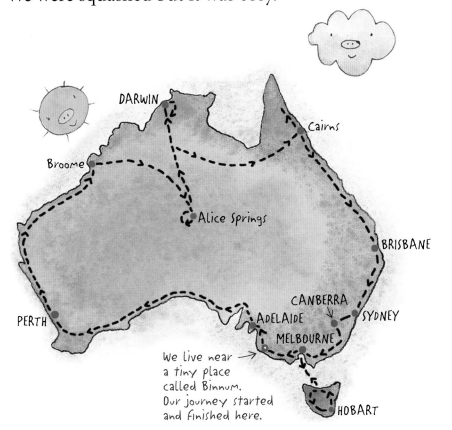

DARWIN
Cairns
Broome
Alice Springs
BRISBANE
CANBERRA
PERTH
ADELAIDE
SYDNEY
MELBOURNE

We live near a tiny place called Binnum. Our journey started and finished here.

HOBART

The day we left, I helped Nan pin up a big map of Australia so she and Poppa could follow our journey.

'I wish I was coming, Grace,' Nan said, as she hugged me tight. 'I'm going to miss our cuddles.'

On the road at last

I waved to Nan and Poppa until Dad turned on to the road leading out to the highway. I felt sad and excited at the same time. Nobody said anything for ages, not until we reached the coast.

We saw the last autumn leaves fluttering like flags on the grapevines of the Barossa Valley.

Then, at the Coorong, Luke made us laugh. 'Look,' he said, 'a pelican. Its beak can hold more than its belly can.'

On our first night we camped on the edge of the Flinders Ranges. It felt like we were the only people in the world.

At Streaky Bay we stuck
our heads in the mouth
of a great white shark.

We made letters with our shadows
at Murphy's Haystacks. The giant
boulders glowed in the afternoon sun.

Keep still, Kylie . . .

That evening at the camping
ground, Mum said Billy
had to use the women's
bathroom because he was
still little. He was embarrassed.
'Okay,' he said, 'but if anyone
comes in, call me Kylie.'

We drove past wheat silos and windmills, and Billy said, 'Are we there yet?'

It took us two days to cross the Nullarbor Plain. I waved to the people in passing cars and trucks, and they always waved back.

We all had our favourite positions in the car.

Dad loved driving →

← Luke rode shotgun

Billy and I shared the middle →

Billyville

Border

Graceland

Mum liked the back where she ↓ could lie down and read

The Great Australian Bight looked like a giant had bitten a huge chunk out of Australia.
Dad and Luke stood right on the edge of the cliff, but Mum stayed back. She held on to Billy and me so tight that my hand went numb.
'Ooh,' she said. 'I can't look.'

At Head of Bight we saw ten whales in the sea below us. A mother and her calf were rolling and wallowing together. Their mournful music sounded like an underwater orchestra. 'It's making me sleepy,' I said to Mum. 'They must be singing a whale lullaby.'

Head of Bight

Over the desert and into the west

At Eucla we had sandy sandwiches near the ruins of the old telegraph station. Next day, we travelled for nearly one hundred and fifty kilometres on a dead-straight road. Dad pretended to drive with his eyes closed, but I could tell he was peeping.

Luke surfed on stone at Wave Rock . . .

. . . but Dad waited for the real waves at Rottnest Island.

The quokkas came so close to me, I could see their tiny whiskers.

After Perth, we went to see the Pinnacles.
They poked up through the sand like
giant limestone fingers.

What we can see

What is hidden underground

What I think the Pinnacles really are

It was so windy at Geraldton that the trees grew sideways.

We drove past a pink tapestry of wildflowers, and Billy said, 'Are we there yet?'

The further north we travelled,
the hotter it became. We stood
in the shallows at Monkey Mia
to see the dolphins.
'Too crowded,' said Dad.
'I liked it better when it was
just us and the whales.'

Mum made me wear
my hat all the time.
'Hats and sunscreen,'
she'd say every time
we stopped. 'This sun
will burn you to a crisp.'

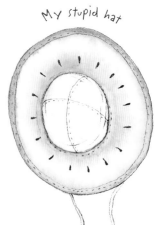

My stupid hat

That afternoon, Mum and Billy and I had a picnic
in the dunes, then fell asleep like a pride of lions.
Later when we went for a dip, a dolphin came up
close and swam right between us.

We went snorkelling at Turquoise Bay.
A gentle current carried us over the coral reef,
as though the ocean was giving us a tour.
There were so many fish, like sparkling jewels.
My favourites were the tiny blue angels.

The Outback

At Broome we ate crunchy fish and chips and watched the moon reflected in the mudflats of Roebuck Bay.
It's called the Staircase to the Moon.

The next day we camped at Windjana Gorge. Mum loved the boab trees. 'They look like opera singers,' she said.
Dad and Luke called them upside-down trees.

We flew over the Bungle Bungles in a helicopter without any doors, and my stomach turned inside out.
'I can't look,' said Mum again.

At Tunnel Creek we waded through an underground river. The dark water came right up to my armpits. When something slimy slithered past my leg, I screamed. Luke said, 'Don't be such a sook.'

Possible creepy things in the water

Heading south on the Tanami Track, the sand was so deep our car got bogged. Everyone felt hot and grouchy, and Mum was worried we'd be stranded in the desert. Luke found a tiny thorny devil, standing fierce as a dragon, and that cheered us up.

A football team helped push us out, and Billy said, 'Are we there yet?'

At Alice Springs we stayed with Mum's friend, Ruth. The days were hot, but the nights were freezing.

Noon

Afternoon

Dusk

Evening

Luke and Billy played footy with some of the local boys.

Ruth took us to her school and a teacher showed Mum and me how to dig for witchetty grubs. They tasted like egg yolk, runny and delicious, with a crunchy head and wriggly legs. Mum wouldn't try one. 'No, thank you,' she said. 'I'm still full from breakfast.'

That afternoon we drove out to see Uluru. Dad spotted it first, when we were still thirty-five kilometres away. 'Wow,' he said. 'That's a BIG rock.' At sunset we watched its colour fade to purple.

We hiked between the round red domes of Kata Tjuta. The trees whispered to us as we walked through the Valley of the Winds.

Uluru is the heart of Australia.
A huge red heart, right in the middle
of the country. One day we got up early
in the cool of the morning, and walked
around the rock. I felt as tiny as an ant.

The Top End

We floated down Katherine Gorge, below towering ochre cliffs. 'This is the life,' said Dad. 'Just wake me up if we come to a waterfall.' We drifted so slowly that even a tortoise swam past us.

We stayed with our cousins in Darwin, and played in their shady pool until we were as wrinkled as prunes.

At night the ceiling fans whirred constantly overhead. Even a sheet felt hot. Tiny grey geckos hunted insects on the walls.

Mum and I loved the market at Mindil Beach. There was so much yummy food, it was hard to choose. We ate satay prawns and drank mango smoothies as we watched the sun set.

We drove across the floodplains, past egrets and jabiru, and Billy said, 'Are we there yet?'

At Kakadu we went on a billabong cruise. The boat drew so close to one enormous crocodile that I could count its teeth.

Luke caught a huge fish in the East Alligator River. It was so big we invited all the other campers to Luke's Barramundi Barbecue.

We swam at Gunlom where there were no saltwater crocodiles. The water was cool and silky. Dad kept diving under and grabbing my feet, and even though I knew it was him, I screamed every time.

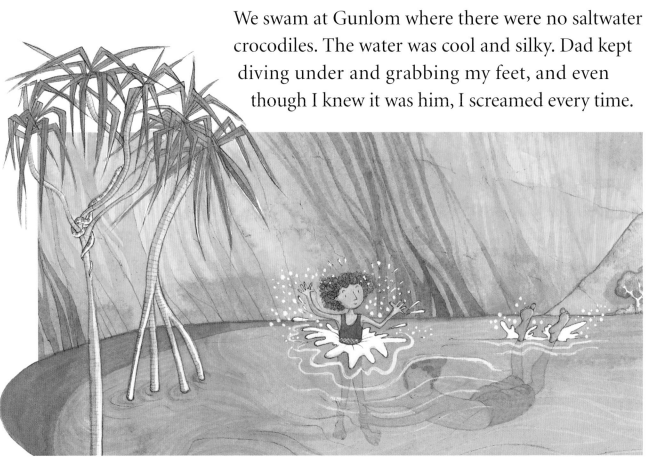

Tony, our Kakadu guide, led us through galleries of rock art. The sandstone overhangs were alive with animals, handprints and spirits from the Dreamtime. Some of the paintings were more than twenty thousand years old. One small handprint looked just like mine.

The Far North

As we travelled on the Barkly Highway, we caught up with a big mob of cattle. We stopped to share our cool water with the dusty drovers, and the boss let me ride his horse for a little way.

Taffy was the same colour as Bess and just as gentle, but twice as tall.

At the circus at Mount Isa, an elephant ate my horrible hat! She swiped it off my head with her trunk and scoffed it. 'Thank you, elephant,' I shouted.

Near Cloncurry the Flying Doctor's plane flew over us. We invented patients for him, and Luke had the best idea: a drover who got bucked off his horse and landed on a spiny anteater.

Dad bought me a new hat at the Mareeba rodeo. 'You look like a real cowgirl, Gracie,' said Mum.

This is the cracker. It makes the noise.

We met an old stockman who taught us how to crack a whip. He showed Luke how to twist the cracker.

That night, Billy and I rode our broncos until they couldn't buck any more.

The next morning, we drove through the shadowy green rainforest, and Billy said, 'Are we there yet?'

In Far North Queensland we
walked beside the Daintree River.
Giant butterflies landed on
Mum's blue T-shirt.
'They think you're a beautiful
flower, Mum,' said Billy.

Luke found a snake-shaped piece of mangrove wood.
He carved it into a walking stick for Poppa.
'I can't look,' said Mum again.

The Great Barrier Reef
was a swirling underwater
carnival of fish and coral.

We went beachcombing at Cow Bay, where the jungle came right down to the sand. Mum and I made a shell mermaid together. 'When the tide comes in tonight, she'll swim out to sea,' said Dad. I imagined her out there, riding her dolphin like an ocean cowgirl.

Cow Bay

Heading south

In Cairns we spent all our time at the pool. One day, Mum crashed into Billy on the water slide and got banned for the whole afternoon.

At Hinchinbrook Island we hiked for hours to swim at Mulligan Falls. That evening, we were so tired and sore we all needed a back rub.

We left the coast and drove inland to visit our friends at Miles. We all helped on the farm, and Luke had a go at shearing. The sheep looked skinny and embarrassed without their wool.

At Surfers Paradise we rode
on a scary bungee ride.
'Uurgh!' moaned Dad, as it
catapulted up. 'I can't look.'
But Mum laughed as she
spun above the lights.
'I *can* look,' she shouted.

Later that week, we caught
heaps of fish off the jetty
at Forster.

OUR FISH

Mum's

Luke's

mine

Dad's

Billy's

Boats skimmed across the sea as we drove down the coast, and Billy said, 'Are we there yet?'

When we got to Sydney we parked our van in Uncle Pete's garden.

Next day at the zoo a baby elephant stared hungrily at my hat so I ran. 'No way,' I yelled. 'I like this hat.'

One day, we went bushwalking in the Blue Mountains. Oil evaporating from the eucalyptus trees makes the blue haze. Mum and I imagined the kind of clothes the Three Sisters would wear.

Uncle Pete's dog, Bongo, towed Luke all the way along Bondi Beach.

Bongo is Buffy's brother

On our last night in Sydney we had a picnic overlooking the harbour. Cascading fireworks exploded across the sky and their reflections shimmered on the water. It felt like a farewell display, just for us.

The Cold Country

On our way to the mountains, we stopped at Canberra and spent a whole day visiting galleries. Mum and I always liked the same paintings.

Billy made a Ned Kelly helmet at Glenrowan. 'Bail up!' he said, 'I'm a bushranger.'

Winter had arrived in the south and it was freezing at Mount Hotham. Billy and Luke and I had never seen snow before. We caught snowflakes in our mouths and wore socks on our hands to keep them warm.

We crossed Bass Strait on a big red ferry. The sea was so rough we all felt sick. Luke turned pale green.

In the Hobart museum we saw a stuffed Tasmanian tiger. I felt sad to think they were extinct. Mum tried to cheer me up. 'You never know, Gracie,' she said. 'There might still be a tiger family in the bush.'

When we went hiking at Cradle Mountain, I kept a lookout for tiger tracks.

It rained so much we played Monopoly for hours. Luke always won, even when Dad and Billy and I ganged up on him.

At the end of the week, we drove back on to the ferry, and Billy said, 'Are we there yet?'

Wilsons Promontory is the most southerly part of the Australian mainland. I found a paper nautilus there, washed ashore at Squeaky Beach.

One evening at Phillip Island, we watched little penguins surf ashore, then waddle up the beach like tiny explorers.

Melbourne was crowded and fast after camping at the beach. The traffic noise kept me awake at night. We learnt to juggle at St Kilda.

On the last day of our trip, Dad got us up early. As we drove away from the city, I looked back at the dawn through sleepy eyes.

Winding along the Great Ocean Road, we stopped to look at the Twelve Apostles standing in the surf. The sea was wild and foaming, and we were nearly home.

The Twelve Apostles

Finally, we were back at our house.
Buffy was so pleased to see us, she jumped right into the car.
I cuddled Tigger and called out to Bess. It was good to hear her whinny back.
Billy woke up and said, 'Are we there yet?'

And we were.
We were home.